D0118691

THRUMP-O-MOTO

JAMES CLAVELL'S
THRUMP

O-MOTO

A Fantasy

DESIGNED & ILLUSTRATED BY
GEORGE SHARP

With Typography by
KEN WILSON

Delacorte Press/New York

Published by
Delacorte Press
1 Dag Hammarskjold Plaza
New York, N.Y. 10017

Also by James Clavell:
KING RAT
TAI-PAN
SHŌGUN
NOBLE HOUSE
THE CHILDREN'S STORY
WHIRLWIND

This work was first published in Great Britain by Hodder and
Stoughton Limited.

Manufactured in Italy

First U.S.A. printing—September 1986

Library of Congress Cataloging-in-Publication Data

Clavell, James.
    James Clavell's Thrump-O-moto.

Summary: When a tiny wizard whisks seven-year-old Patricia and
her crutches from her home in Australia to Japan, she encounters
the wizard's family, an evil ghoul, and the hope of a magic cure for
her physical handicap.

    [1. Physically handicapped—Fiction. 2. Japan—Fiction.
3. Australia—Fiction. 4. Fantasy] I. Sharp, George, ill.
II. Title. III. Title: Thrump-O-moto.
PZ7.C5737Th   1986   [E]
ISBN 0-385-29504-9
Library of Congress Catalog Card Number: 86-4485

H E WALKED OUT OF THE RAMBLING house with the little girl in his arms and settled her in her chair that was in the shade of the great jacaranda tree. 'There you are, luv. Bye for now.'

'Bye, Dad. Are you mustering again today?'

'No, darling. Today Old Charlie's overseeing the sheep,' he said, smiling down at her, loving her, the early morning sun hot and the shade sweet. Beyond and all around the land was flat, vast, the edge of the Australian Outback, scrubland, good for sheep but not so good for cattle. 'I'm going over to the north section. Some of the cattle have been straying. I'll be back by teatime. You all right now?'

'Oh yes,' she said though she didn't want him to leave. It was lonely with no one to play with, Dad gone all day and Mum always working. 'You're sure you'll be home for tea?'

'Too right,' he said with the laugh she loved so much. 'Today we've your favourite, kippers all the way

[2]

from England, just like Grandad used to have. Mum went to the store especially and she'll bake a loaf for hot buttered toast. 'Bye, Little Girl.'

'Good-oh!' She felt the roughness of his skin as he kissed her and smelled his grand, warm man-smell. Then he tousled her hair and walked away, tall and strong, his old jeans and shirt and battered old hat sweatstained. She craned around in her chair to watch him get into the jeep, her tears very near.

'No,' she muttered to herself, 'no tears and think good thoughts, like Dad says.'

She waved to him bravely but he was already through the big wooden gates that ran between their house and paddocks and sheep and cattle pens. Their house was single storey, low and rambling with outhouses, barns and lean-tos, the roof part tiled and part corrugated iron that made a noise like thunder during the Wet. Near the house were a few flower beds. But here there was little time to tend flowers.

I wish I could do that for Mum, she thought. Kippers? Well, they're not really my favourite but Dad loves them so much, just like Grandad did, so I don't mind. 'Spaghetti's really my favourite,' she said out loud.

She settled back in her chair and began to wait.

Now she could hear her mother in the kitchen, cleaning the pots and pans from breakfast, singing as she worked. Always cleaning and cooking and getting water from the roof tank or making the beds or washing. And Dad always working and driving and coming home and eating and laughing with Mum and me and oh, how lucky we are!

It was cool in the shade, the flies not bad in this season—springtime—and she knew that soon her mother would bring some more lemonade and they would begin a lesson or two. She let her mind drift, watching herself run after the jeep that was now just a dustcloud on the horizon. I'd run and run and then, when I was tired, I'd walk to the creek and swim and have such a lovely time. I'd jump in the water and splash and sing, then I'd dry myself and walk home and th—

A sudden noise startled her. She came out of her reverie and looked up into the lower branches of the jacaranda tree. What seemed to be a ball of multicoloured material tumbled to the earth below, then the ball untangled itself with coughs and splutters and became the strangest tiny little boy.

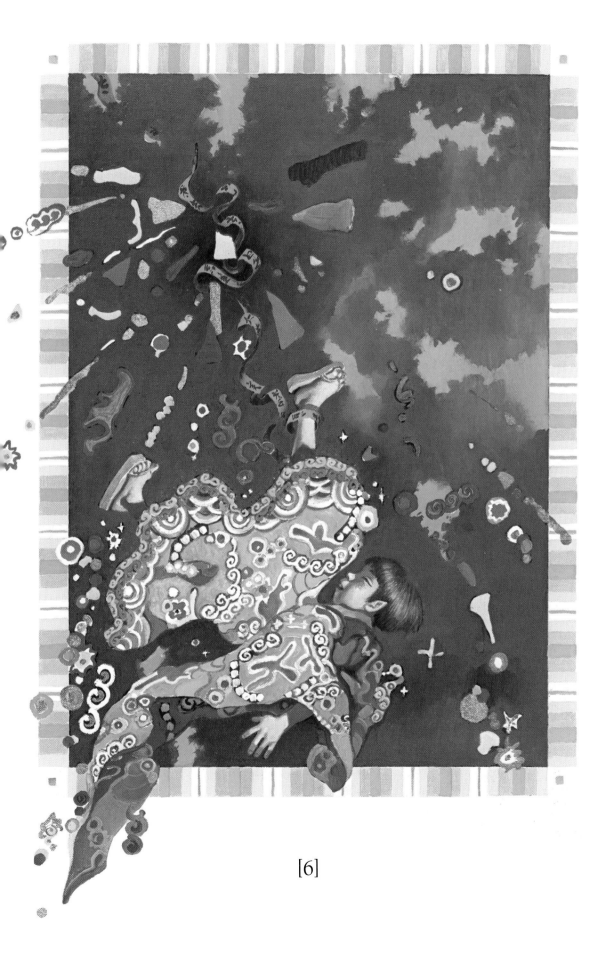

[6]

'Oh! G'day,' she gasped. 'Who're you?'

'I'm Thrump-O-moto,' the tiny boy said breathlessly, brushed the leaves and twigs off hastily, adjusted his robe that almost seemed just a little too big for him then bowed with vast aplomb. 'Please excuse me for arriving like this! I'm really discombobulated.'

'What?'

'Oh! It's the new word I've just learned from my English teacher. It means I really have lost much face by falling out of your tree.' He beamed up at her and mopped his brow. He was scarcely two feet high and dressed in a kimono, a long, belted multicoloured robe with two carved wooden sticks stuck into the belt, one longer than the other. His slanting eyes were dark and twinkling, his hair black and skin a pleasing golden colour. 'I'm a wizard, at least, to be honest, my Ka-chan's a wizardess and she says that when I'm grown up I'm going to be the best wizard in Japan.'

'That's wonderful. A wizard?' She shifted in her chair to see him better. 'You're very lucky to be a wizard. What's Ka-chan?'

'It means Mother or Ma or Mum or Mummy in Japanese.' Thrump-O-moto gathered his kimono around him and knelt in the grass, the grass now almost hiding him. 'I'm Japanese too.'

'Ah, now I understand. But, but your Ka-chan, your Mum, she's really a wizardess—a *real* wizardess?'

'Oh yes, to be honest my Ka-chan's quite a super wizardess. May I ask your name, please?'

'Patricia. Patricia's my real name but my Dad and Mum they call me Luv or Darling or Darling Heart or Little Girl.'

'Hummm!' Thrump-O-moto peered up at her then he smiled. 'I like Pat-ri-cia better than the other names. May I ask how old you are, please?'

'I'm almost eight.'

'I'm four hundred and sixty-five.'

He beamed up at her. 'Of course wizards count differently.'

'They do?' She thought a moment. 'You don't look much older than me.'

'Four hundred and sixty-five by wizard's count about eight by yours,' he said.

She frowned. 'Are you sure you're a wizard, Mister, er, I mean you are rather small to be a wizard and you wear such funny clothes.'

'Oh I'm only small because you're small—compared to your Dad and Mum but, to be honest, I can be very big if I want to. Oh yes, very big indeed.'

'Really, Mister, er—'

'Thrump-O-moto. Oh yes, indeed and these clothes aren't really funny. They're just different. They're called kimonos, Miss Pat-ri-cia. This is how people dress in Japan, particularly wizards.'

'You do look very handsome,' she said happily. 'Do girls dress like that too?'

'Yes, yes they do but their kimonos are a little different.' He glanced at her house with its outhouses and pens. 'Do you have brothers and sisters?'

'No. No I don't. Not yet.'

'I don't either,' he said.

She studied him and decided she really liked him. 'I'm very pleased to meet you, Mr. Thrump-O-moto, and very glad you've come to visit me. Yes, I'm ever so pleased to meet you.' She reached down with her hand and he got up and shook her first finger which was all his own hand could encircle.

'Thank you, and I'm very pleased to meet you too'. Thrump-O-moto bowed again then looked around. The land went to the horizon. Few trees.

[10]

Flocks of strange birds whirled this way and that and there was a smell on the wind different to that at home. Now he was clearly worried. 'May I ask where we are? I mean where in the world? You see I really shouldn't be here because I was practising a trick to visit my grand-oba-chan at the seaside and there's no seaside and clearly we're not in Japan.'

'Oh dear, poor Mr. Thumpamoto. You're a long wa—'

'Thrump-O-moto,' he said gravely. 'So sorry, Miss Pat-ri-cia, but wizards have to be called by their real name.'

'I'm sorry,' she said. 'But I've never met a wizard before. Well, Mr. *Thrump*-O-moto, I think you're a very long way from Japan. Oh yes, I remember seeing Japan in my atlas. Japan's a long way north, across the sea, up alongside China. Now you're in Australia. Down Under.'

'Pardon? Down under what?'

Again she laughed and he felt warmed by it and some of his fear left him. 'That's Aussie, that's what old people sometimes call Australia. "Down Under", because it's down under the rest of the world.'

'Oh! For a moment, to be honest, you scared me. Australia? I did really get my trick higgle-deediggledeemoted.' His worry increased. 'Is Down Under a big country, Miss Pat-ri-cia?'

'The biggest in the world! The best in the world!'

'But such a long way from home, oh-dinimoto!'

'You mustn't be worried. You must be a very big wizard indeed to come all the way here by yourself so you can easily wizz your way back if you want.'

'You're sure, really sure?' She nodded and his worry vanished in the sun of her smile. 'Oh thank you very much, Miss Pat-ri-cia. But we call it "wozzing" to wozz here and wozz there.'

'Oh. Well please don't wozz, please don't go home yet, Mr. Thrump-O-moto. I know, let's be friends. Then you don't have to call me Miss and I'll drop the Mister'.

'Very indeed excellent! And . . . and . . .' He went right up to her, barely as tall as her knees and put out

his tiny hand again. 'And as we're friends you can call me Thrump-O-moto for short.'

'But that's not short at all,' she said.

'Oh but it is for a wizard,' he said and nodded vigorously. 'Of course at home sometimes I'm called Thrump-O, or just "O". Would that be better?'

'Thrump-O is nice. O's nice too. I'll try both.' She leaned down and carefully offered her first finger and again he shook it. 'Now we're friends.'

'Very good. Please, Pat-ri-cia, just exactly where are we?'

'Well-O, you're at our station, that's like a farm or a ranch. It's called Moonside near Muldoon Crossing, that's where the store and the post office are. Our nearest town is Madorah and we're on the edge of the Outback—that's what we call the far country, far away from the coast.' Patricia's eyes were dreamy. 'I saw the sea once. It was so pretty. Would you like some lemonade? It's cool and sweet. My Mum makes it.' She reached under her chair and brought out the thermos and offered it.

'That's very tasty,' he said, drinking out of the cup. 'Thank you. We have lemonade in Japan too. To be honest, I'm very fond of lemonade. Could we go for a walk?'

'Certainly, if you'd like to, but not too far.' She reached down in the tall grass and found her crutches.

'What're those for?' he asked.

'They help me walk. I call them Twiddle-dee-dee and Twiddle-dee-bang 'cause this one's always falling down with a bang. You see, when I was very little, about three years ago, I got a very bad illness. I was very sick and afterwards my legs didn't work.'

'Oh dear, poor Miss Pat-ri-cia.' Thrump-O-moto shuddered in the warmth of the sun. 'Oh yes,' he said. 'We know of that bad spirit at home too. We wizards call him Nurk-u the Bad.'

'Yes, he's very bad but my dad said one day I'll be able to run if I'm quiet and wait and think good thoughts.' She lifted herself painfully and put her crutches under her armpits and smiled down at Thrump-O-moto. 'Let's go to the end of the garden'

'You're sure it's all right for you, Pat-ri-cia?'

'Oh yes. Every day I must try, that's what my Dad says. But we must watch out for snakes—sometimes they hide in the grass.'

So they set off slowly, Thrump-O-moto just a little ahead to see there was no danger. At the end of the garden was a tiny pool and a little mound and he ran up to it and looked all around. His worry increased. 'It really is very big and … and not a hill or house anywhere, anywhere at all.'

'Our neighbours aren't far away, just half a day's ride if my Dad drives. My Dad's Manager of Moonside. It's not very big, just a day by jeep that way and two days by jeep that way.'

'That's very very to be honest huge!'

'No, O. Here it's quite small. We've about thirty thousand head of sheep, two or three hundred cattle and in good years, lots and lots of wheat.' She leaned on her crutches. 'What's Japan like?'

'Very, very different from this.'

'Oh, I'd just love to see Japan!'

All at once there was a great rushing of wind and she felt herself speeding skywards and she gasped and shut her eyes.

O H MY', SHE GASPED. NOW SHE WAS in Japan, beside the sea. Nearby was the strangest, prettiest little village with fishermen and boats and little girls and boys playing on the beach and lots and lots of laughter. 'We're in Japan,' she cried out excitedly. 'How did you do that, O?'

'Well, you see "Oh, I'd just love to . . ." to a wizard is a magic sentence to grant a wish.'

'Oh! You mean if I say "Oh, I'd . . ."' She stopped herself just in time. 'If I say the magic sentence you'll grant my wish every time?'

'Oh no,' he said. 'I can't because, to be honest, I'm not a real wizard yet. And even with real wizards or wizardesses it only works sometimes. I don't quite know, to be honest, how that trick works.'

'Can we get back home, Thrump-O? I mean . . .' She became a little worried. 'I really must be home by teatime.'

'When's that?'

'Just before sunset. Like everyone.' She frowned. 'Don't you have teatime, when you eat the big meal of the day—after work?'

'No, no we eat differently.' He grinned. 'Don't you worry, Pat-ri-cia. Ka-chan can get you home by your teatime. But first I'll take you to our home to meet her.' He beamed up at her. 'That was a good trick, wasn't it, Pat-ri-cia, to wozz you to Japan in . . . poof, the blink of a lightning.'

'Oh yes-O!' Then she noticed that everyone and everything was his size—tiny—and she was almost like a giantess. 'But-O, I'm so tall and you're so small —can I come down to your size? Please.'

'Certainly, Pat-ri-cia.' He made a magic sign and said some magic words that she could not understand. 'Pull the lobe of your left ear, quick!' he ordered.

She obeyed and all at once she felt a pat on her head and she was shrinking, shrinking, shrinking and now they were the same size. 'Oh-O! You really are a super wizard, O.'

Wide-eyed, she looked around. The small wooden houses were grouped together with roofs of

[21]

[22]

blue clay tiles and every house with a little garden and all of them fenced and nothing like she had ever seen before. Boats were in neat lines and fishermen repaired nets. Southward, the harbour was well protected by headlands. Overhead were billowing clouds and gentle sun and gulls cawed and played over the surf frothing up the beach. Beyond the surf the blue green sea was dotted with islands, big and small and tiny. To the north were high hills and beyond them mountains—all beautiful dark green with tall trees and wild flowers everywhere. 'It's so pretty, O. I've never seen anything so pretty. I've always wanted to live near the sea. Which way should we go?'

'This way. Mind the stones. They may be slippery.' He led the way down the rise, through the boys and girls playing in the shallows and on the beach.

'G'day,' she said politely but no one paid her any attention. 'What's wrong with everyone, O?'

'Ah, so sorry, Pat-ri-cia, they can't see you or hear you. Only wizards and spirits can see you and hear you. But there's nothing to be worried about,' he added seeing her concern. 'I'll look after you.'

'Oh, thank you, Thrump-O. To be honest, I'm not afraid so long as you're here.'

'That's what friends are for,' he said.

She rested for a moment, watching the children play in the surf. 'Then this is like a dream—like *dreamtime*?'

'Oh no, it certainly isn't.' He reached over and pinched her lightly. 'There, you see! This is the real-est time ever!'

'Good-oh!' she told him contentedly, reassured, and started along the path again.

After a little while he stopped at a lovely house made of wood, with walls of wooden laths with squares of paper in them and many strange pots of brilliant flowers everywhere. A path of flat stones led to a door, also made of wood and paper. He slid it aside, kicked off his shoes and rushed inside.

'Ka-chan, Ka-chan watachi desu,' he called out. But because he was a wizard and the little girl was in his spell she understood his Japanese as though it was English and did not notice any difference. 'Mother, it's me!' he had said.

'Where have you been, my son? I've been

looking everywhere for you and . . . oh!' The beautiful woman stopped, startled to see the little girl in her doorway. She wore a shimmering pink kimono with fishes embroidered on it and her hair was dark and long and tied up. Inside and out the house was spotless with no furniture anywhere except for a few cushions and very low tables. The floor was covered with strange and beautiful matting. 'Who's this?'

'This is Pat-ri-cia from Australia,' Thrump-O-moto said importantly. 'I wozzed her to visit us.'

'Ah, from Australia! Well done, my son. You're very welcome Pat-ri-cia. Please come in and sit down, but first let me take your shoes off.' She knelt and helped the little girl out of them. 'It's our custom not to wear shoes in the house. It keeps the house clean.'

'What a good idea, Mrs. Thrump-O-moto! That'd save my Mum such a lot of work. Everything's so neat and different! Not like our station at all!'

'Her station's bigger than the hugest farm in all Japan,' Thrump-O-moto said.

'Ah, is that so? My name is Minamoto-thrump-O-moto but you may call me Ka-chan. Would you like tea?'

'Yes, yes please, Ka-chan.' As she sat awkwardly on a cushion on the mat-like floor one of the crutches slipped out of her hand and fell down but Thrump-O-moto caught it.

'Twiddle-dee-bang didn't bang that time,' he said with a laugh, then explained about the names of the crutches to his mother.

'Ah, now I understand. So sorry you've been ill, child. Now, let's have some tea.' Ka-chan clasped her hands and said strangely, 'Spirits, spirits hear my words: Minamoto-thrumpomoto-minamoto-thrump-omotooooooh! We would like tea, please!'

And lo and behold an exquisite little teapot appeared on a tray with three matching little cups with no handles. The little girl clapped her hands with delight. 'Can you teach me to do that, Ka-chan?'

'In time, Pat-ri-cia. In the spirit's time.' Ka-chan poured the tea. It was green, delicate and very different.

'I've never had tea like this before, Ka-chan. We drink ours with milk and sugar and the tea's dark and not green.'

'Oh. I've never had your tea either. Is this all right for you, Pat-ri-cia? Really?'

'Oh yes.'

'Please but, ah so sorry, I've never met an Australian person before. Would you please tell me about your home and your life?'

The little girl told her, warmed by her and feeling very much at home. Then Thrump-O-moto told

how they had got here and how his first trick had gone wrong.

Ka-chan chided him gently. 'You forgot to pull the lobe of your right ear after you said the magic words. In a few minutes I have to visit Grandfather Ten. We'll go together and I'll show you again and then, on the way back, you can practise and you won't get lost again.'

'May I go too, please, Ka-chan?' the little girl asked.

'Of course, of course you can.'

'Ka-chan,' Thrump-O-moto said, 'could we, just this once, could we let her leave her sticks behind. She is sort of in a spell and, to be honest, Pat-ri-cia has difficulty. Could you make another spell, please, for Pat-ri-cia.'

Ka-chan thought a moment. Then she said, 'Well-O, Pat-ri-cia can leave her crutches here for just this once but she'll need a walking stick.' She went inside the house and came back with an old, gnarled stick. 'This belonged to my great grandfather. This will help you, child. But, take care, because magic needs help too. Now we all hold hands and say the magic words and we touch the right lobe of our ears. Ready?'

'Yes,' they both replied and the little girl was so excited.

'Spirits, spirits hear my words: Minamoto-thrumpomoto-minamoto-thrumpomoto . . .' Then Ka-chan added some secret magic words. They each touched their right earlobe and all at once they

[31]

[32]

were in a great forest in the mountains with wonderful tall trees and soft glades beside a little waterfall that spilled from the heavens into a clear stream. Across the stream was a curved bridge and, beside it, a cottage with blue-green tiles and flowers everywhere. Smoke came from a little fire that was outside in the garden. Over the fire was a big cauldron.

'Here we are', Ka-chan said. 'Come along. Are you all right, Pat-ri-cia?'

'Well, I think so'. Timidly she made a tiny tentative step. It felt very strange, very strange indeed but she stood firm. Another step, then another. The stick took most of her weight.

'You're doing very well, Pat-ri-cia,' Thrump-O-moto said encouragingly though he was very concerned. 'How do you feel?'

'Wonderful', the little girl said gloriously, watching her feet go one after another, just like other children, with only a little tingling and a little strangeness in her legs. 'Oh this is wonderful Ka-chan!' But just as she reached the centre of the bridge the sky darkened and a chill wind began to

tear at their clothes. Then, out of the sudden mist, they all heard the sound of crashing branches. The sounds got louder and louder, approaching. The two children huddled into Ka-chan's skirts.

'What is it, what's happening?' the little girl cried out.

'Quick . . . quick, we must run'. Ka-chan lifted her into her arms and, with Thrump-O-moto, fled before the noise. But the noise followed. They ran harder and all the time the wind grew stronger, tearing at them, trying to stop them. On and on, through the forest, down the valleys, up the hills, across the bridges, along the rice fields, up the winding mountain path, leaves and flower petals torn by the grasping wind, swirling about them. Suddenly the path vanished and there was only the cliff before them.

'Oh dear-O-dreadful-moto! We're trapped!' Ka-chan said.

'Who is it—what is it?' Patricia held on to her stick.

Then out of the forest came the great cruel voice. 'It's me! Nurk-u the Bad!'

The little girl gasped. Trees were torn aside. The earth shook. Nurk-u stood as high as the heavens and he was dressed all in fire with five eyes and blue hair and ten fingers on each hand, his nails like long knives. Green poison dropped from the tips.

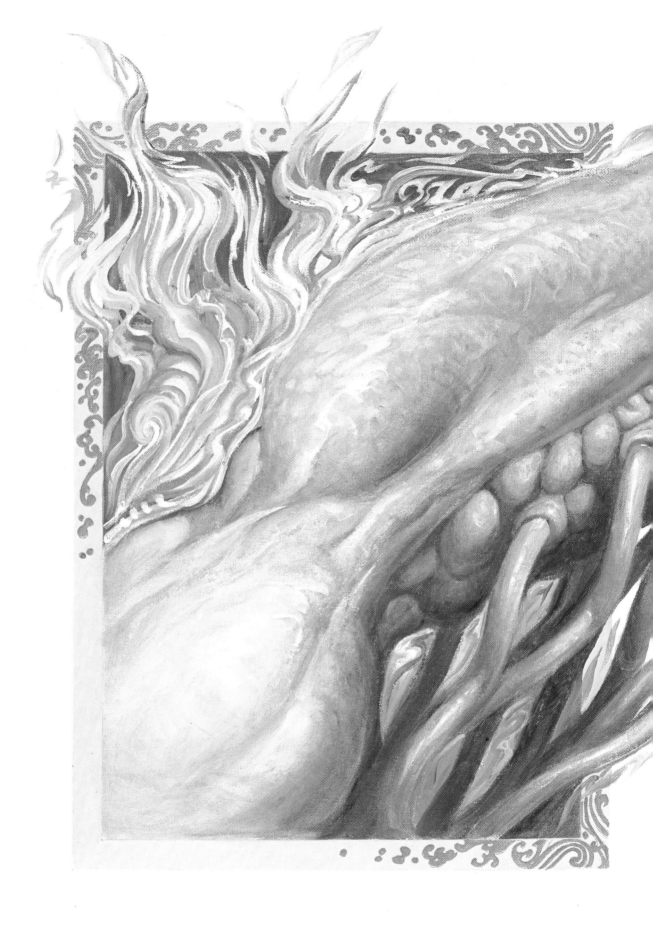

'You awful monster! Go away!' she
cried, terrified.

'I don't want you, Little Girl, I've got you!
It's Thrump-O-moto I've come for!' Nurk-u
the Bad growled, his voice filling the great
ravine below and the crags above. 'Come here, boy!'

'No, no, you can't have O!' Patricia shouted
out and hobbled towards him with her stick, even
though she was very frightened. 'You go away or
I'll call my dad and he'll knock you down!'

[38]

But all Nurk-u the Bad did was to roar with laughter. The blast of his breath knocked the little girl to the ground. She tried to struggle to her feet. Behind her Ka-chan shouted, 'Quickly, my son, defend yourself, defend her, you must fight this battle yourself. But don't let him touch you with his nails!'

At once, Thrump-O-moto rushed forward. He helped Patricia to her feet then whirled on Nurk-u the Bad. Trying to contain his fear, he waved his hands making all the magic signs he knew and called out in his piping little voice: 'All spirits great and small hear my words! Thrumpo-moto-ozimoto-nasimoto-every-moto!' then added the special magic words that can only be said and not written and he began to grow and grow until now he was the same size as Nurk-u the Bad, the little sticks in his belt became swords and he tore at the monster with a great shout.

And now the battle raged on the cliff edge.

Each swung at the other but both missed. They circled, waiting for an opening. Suddenly Nurk-u lashed out. The ghoul's nails ripped Thrump-O-moto's kimono but oh so luckily the poisoned claws did not touch his skin as he darted backwards.

Again they circled, waiting for an opening, then O side-stepped and smote the monster with all his strength. His sword sang through the air and lopped off the monster's head. But the battle was not won and they all groaned aloud as, at once, another head more ugly then the last grew in its place. Instead of five eyes, now there were ten and great barbs all over his body.

Nurk-u the Bad was exploding with rage and he howled, 'I'll teach you a lesson, Thrump-O-moto!' He hurtled forward in a rush that carried the youth to the very brink of the cliff.

Ka-chan and the little girl were aghast. Thrump-O-moto teetered there, almost lost, on the very edge, but with a great effort he recovered his balance and when Nurk-u

leapt at him again he twisted aside
and struck at the enemy. The blow
was good and he lopped off one of
the monster's arms but the arm
sprouted back at once, bigger
than before.

'You'll never beat me, never!'
Nurk-u shouted. The earth shook as
he stamped with rage. Undaunted, the
youth held his ground, circling, then
again charged. But this time he
was careless. The sword was torn
out of his hands and he stumbled.

At once Nurk-u hacked down-
wards. Desperately Patricia shouted
a warning. At the very last
second Thrump-O heard her
and he whirled, leapt to his feet,
darted away, then without any
warning charged back to the
attack. He caught the monster
around the chest, pinning his
arms to his sides.

They struggled on the very edge of the cliff. The earth began to give way.

'Go on-O,' Patricia shouted, encouraging him though she was terribly afraid and so tiny against their hugeness. 'You've got to win-O!'

'Hold on, my son! Hold on for your life,' Ka-chan called out.

'Win,' the little girl cried out with all her strength. 'Win-O, I know you can!'

They watched helplessly. The battle went on and on. Still Thrump-O held Nurk-u pinioned. But now he was tiring. They knew the end was near. Then Nurk-u cunningly pretended to slip but instead he twisted and the youth was almost jerked off his feet. Immediately Nurk-u the Bad saw the opening. His poisoned nails got closer and closer, closer and closer. But Thrump-O had tricked him and now had him off balance. With a last mighty effort, he lifted the howling ghoul off his feet and hurled him off the cliff.

'Oh how clever of you-O!' Patricia shouted gleefully. 'You thrumped him, you thrumped him! Good-O, Good-O!'

'Well done, my son, well done!'

'Oh thank you, Mother, thank you Pat-ri-cia.' Thrump-O-moto peered down at them, the sweat running off him in a great river, his breath coming in great gasps that sounded like a whirlwind. 'Are you both all right?'

'Oh yes, oh yes!'

'Well done, my son!' Ka-chan was so pleased with him. 'To be honest, that was very well done indeed. Perhaps you'd better come down to our size now.'

'Oh so sorry,' he said. 'But Ka-chan, I need some help.'

In a moment he was his normal size once more and again they congratulated him. Ka-chan made very sure there was not even the tiniest scratch anywhere. As an added protection she said a few magic words. 'But you protected yourself, my son. And protected us too. Unfortunately, even for wizards, there are times when you—you alone—can fight certain fights. Well done again. Now come along, we're safe now.'

So they started back and, because the walking stick that the little girl had was a magic walking

stick, now she found she
could walk quite well
without leaning on it
too much. 'Oh how
wonderful!' My legs feel
funny, Ka-chan, but I
think I can manage.'

'Take care, Pat-ri-cia,'
Ka-chan cautioned her.
'A little at a time
and remember always
carry the walking stick
with you.'

'I won't forget,
Ka-chan.'

'Good. Walk a little
more each day and who
knows? After all, you were
very brave too that's
very important. Wasn't
she, my son?'

'Oh yes.'

Happily they went back

[46]

the way they had come, taking their time and letting the little girl rest as she wanted. Now the sun shone on them and the birds and the insects welcomed them. So did Grandfather Kazimoto-minamoto-toramoto-maximoto-thrump-O-moto-ten. 'But you can call me Ten. You see, Miss Pat-ri-cia, I'm the Tenth Wizard in the family,' he said gravely.

'Yes,' Ka-chan said. 'And the wisest.'

'Not the wisest.' The old man chuckled and held his big stomach, 'but certainly the thirstiest.' He poured some sake into tiny cups and offered one to Patricia. 'Try just a taste. It's like wine. We always drink it warm.'

She took a sip. Her nose wrinkled. 'I think I'll have to wait till I grow up, Grandfather Ten. I don't like beer either.'

They talked and talked and he congratulated them all on their escape. 'Nurk-u the Bad is very, very wicked. Few escape him, and if so much as one of his claws scratches you . . . dear-O-dinimoto, you get the sickness.'

'Yes,' Patricia said. 'Yes, that's true. I can't remember Nurk-u the Bad scratching me but I'm awfully glad he didn't touch you-O, and awfully glad to be here. I had such a lovely time coming back, I've quite forgotten Twiddle-dee-dee and Twiddle-dee-bang!' She explained about her crutches to Grand-father Ten.

'Ah, now I understand,' he said.

'Grandfather,' Thrump-O-moto began. 'Is there a magic drink or spell against Nurk-u the Bad? I mean, even after he's scratched a person. I mean for Pat-ri-cia?'

'Yes and no, child, no and yes.' The old Wizard frowned and studied her. She felt her heart go thumpettythump thumpettythump.

'She's certainly been very brave and that's the first part of the magic,' he said. 'But . . .' He was silent a long time.

'What about zu-nu-xu-plonk-u?' Ka-chan asked.

'No, Ka-chan, I'm afraid that wouldn't be any good in this case. Let's eat a little and I'll drink a little and I'll think a lot.'

And so they did. The sun went down. A day and a night passed and another day. The little girl was

quite content because they explained that woz-time was different from ordinary time, very different indeed. So she played in the stream and swam and every day she walked a little better so that soon she just carried the stick with her and no longer needed to lean on it. Around the fire at night she told them stories about her home and about how, one day, she and her Dad and Mum would fly all around the world. 'Of course I'd rather woz like you do,' she said.

'Wozzing is very nice. When you do it right.'

Thrump-O-moto sighed. 'You have to work very hard to be a wizard. School's very hard.'

She sighed too. 'It's the same for me, O. At home school's quite far away and as . . . as I can't walk very far, sometimes I learn at home, and don't have anyone to play with either. But my Mum and Dad teach me so I don't ever fall behind.'

'Without friends, life can be very difficult,' Ka-chan said and gave her a hug. But now you've us as friends.'

And so they talked the days and nights and had many adventures. Then one day when the sun was going down they heard a call: 'Thrump-O-motoooh!'

'It's Grandfather Ten! Perhaps he has the spell for you! I'll race you,'

Thrump-O-moto said.

By this time the little girl could even run. So they raced, Ka-chan's magic stick in her hand, and she won and they were both very happy.

'Yes Grandfather?' he asked expectantly.

'Sunset Primroses!' the old man burst out. 'That's it! Essence of Sunset Primroses! That's the answer! ESP! With ESP and a magic word or two, lots of courage, much patience and a pull at your right earlobe and kozzzimoto-ooooh! It should work!'

'Good, oh very, very good, Grandfather Ten!' Thrump-O said so happily. 'But where do we get Essence of Sunset Primroses?'

'I'm afraid I don't know. We'll have to

ask Ka-chan,' the Old Wizard said. 'She must look into the Magic Pool!'

They ran out and found her in the garden. 'Please, please hurry, Ka-chan,' Thrump-O-moto begged her. 'Let's go at once.'

'I will go at once children,' she said immediately, hiding her great fear from them. 'But I must go alone. There are many things in life one must do alone and this is one. Only one person can look into the Magic Pool at one time. After supper, when you're both fast asleep, I'll wozz to the land of Xanadu where Kubla Khan a stately pleasure dome decreed and Alph the sacred river runs through caverns measureless to man down to a boundless sea. There I'll l—'

'Sorry, but I don't understand, Ka-chan,' the little girl said. 'Where's Xanadu?'

'That's where I must go. Beyond the setting sun. I must go alone to Xanadu. Now,' Ka-chan added, changing the subject, 'tonight we will have fresh grilled fish and rice and . . .' She told them the meal she had prepared but her mind was on her journey. It would be long and hard and dangerous. Never mind, she thought. I will make the journey for Patricia . . .

[56]

The quest took her a year and a day and Gangee the Witch tried to stop her and so did Forty-Headed Fu but she slipped by them and came home safely.

'I'm so happy to see you, Ka-chan,' the little girl said, hugging her. 'We were all so worried. Are you all right?'

'Yes, yes thank you,' Ka-chan replied very happily, so pleased to see them too. 'But I am very hungry, I've hardly eaten anything since I left.'

At once Patricia rushed into the kitchen and brought fresh rice and other things that she had just cooked. In Ka-chan's absence she had learned to cook and to clean—and the house was spotless. By now she didn't even have to carry her walking stick. She just stuck it into the belt around her waist. Now she wore a kimono that Grandfather Ten had given her.

'This tastes very good, Pat-ri-cia!' Ka-chan said, pleased with her progress. 'Now I think I will rest awhile, but wake me when Grandfather Ten returns.'

That evening when Grandfather Ten returned and the little girl had given him warm *sake*, Ka-chan began: 'Essence of Sunset Primrose comes from a flower which is different from the little primrose but also has the lovely sparkling golden flower you find in many places, good places and some wild places, all over the world. But the special Sunset Primrose to cure Nurk-u the Bad's sickness for Pat-ri-cia comes from a place called Eng-land and—'

'I know about England,' the little girl burst out. 'That's where my Grandad came from!'

'That's a great help, Pat-ri-cia,' Ka-chan said. 'Now in all the land of Eng-land there's only one special glade for you, so I was told, and the glade belongs to a strong wizard called Charley Rednosebeerdrinker.'

'Old Rednosebeerdrinker! I know him!' Grandfather Ten went very red in the face and upset his little cup in his excitement. 'I met him at our reunion, oh about eight hundred and twenty years ago.'

'My goodness,' Patricia said. 'That is a very long time ago, Grandfather Ten.'

'Yes, but it's not long for a wizard. It's like yesterday, Pat-ri-cia,' he said. 'Now wait a moment, I think I have his name card somewhere.' At length he found it. 'Hummmmmm! The magic glade is in the south of England at Friendly Manor where there is a faerie ring and

Charles Rednosebeerdrinker Esq.
——
FRIENDLY MANOR
ENGLAND

a huge tree, a kami tree. A kami's a good spirit, Pat-ri-cia. But oh-dinimoto, it seems I can't go and Ka-chan can't go . . .'

'I'll go,' Thrump-O-moto said at once. 'I'll go.'

'But it may be difficult and there are dangers.'

'I'm not afraid. Please, for Pat-ri-cia.'

'But, O, if there's danger, then you mustn't go. You've battled enough for us already. I'm afraid for you-O.'

'Huh! I'll find the Sunset Primrose for you. I'll go after supper.'

'Well, O,' Patricia said. 'Let's go together. That's only fair.'

And they argued. But nicely. Then they agreed. Ka-chan solved everything: just this once, for just this one journey, the little girl would become an apprentice wizardess.

'Oh thank you,' she said and clapped her hands with delight. 'I'd love to be a wizardess.'

'Then you are one! You said the first of the magic words yourself! But you must take your stick with you,' Ka-chan said.

'Oh yes, I will. And I promise not to lose it.'

So Grandfather Ten said the other magic words and made the magic signs and waved his magic wand. 'There!'

'Oh!'

'Now you're an apprentice wizardess!'

'But I don't feel any different, Grandfather Ten. Can I do a trick?'

'Not yet, Pat-ri-cia,' Grandfather Ten said, 'O has to teach you.' He gave them advice and instructions, then added, 'Now off you go and remember, Pat-ri-cia, when the sky gets very dark and the wind howls and the nasties of the earth come after you, just puff and huff and call out: Minamoto-kazimoto-finklemoto-Patriciamotoooooooh—and all will be well. But don't forget that the magic's only good for one time so be careful. And always do what Thrump-O says.'

Again she promised. Then they went on to the bridge, to the very centre.

'Good luck, O—good luck, Patriciamoto! Come back quickly.' Grandfather Ten, the old Wizard and Ka-chan, the Wizardess, waved goodbye. Thrump-O-moto said the magic words and they wozzed.

'H THAT WAS QUICK!' SHE SAID. The wood was so gentle. It was near sunset. The sun filtered through the leaves and made them all pink and gold. Nearby was a quiet stream. Birds played in the boughs and called, one to another. And all around was a carpet of yellow flowers, rustled by the breeze. 'Are these Sunset Primroses?' she asked breathlessly.

'Course they is,' a voice rasped. Startled, they whirled around. No one was anywhere to be seen.

'Mr. Charley Rednosebeerdrinker? Is that you?'

'Of course it's me. An' who might you be?'

'I'm Thrump-O-moto and this is Pat-ri-cia and Grandfather Ten sent us.'

'Old Ten?' There was a great chuckle. 'Old Ten, eh? How is my old mate?'

'He's very well, thank you,' Thrump-O-moto said.

'Good-oh!' The rotund little man came out from under a fallen tree, a beer mug in his hand, his long coat and tight trousers were patched and not very

clean at all and his top hat was bent
and busted and perched on his head. His
eyes were twinkling eyes and his nose big
and very red. First he took a swig of beer
then he beamed up at her. 'Wot can I do for you?'

Together they told him and where they had
come from.

'Humm,' he said and sipped some beer.
'You're English, Pat me girl?'

'I'm Aussie,' she replied politely. 'My
Grandad came from London.'

'Aussie, eh? I was Down Under
once meself, on me holiday. Humm!
So you want some of me ESP.
Supplies is short, this time
of the year.'

'Oh yes, please.'

'Oh yes, yes please, if
you could spare some,' Thrump-O-moto
echoed. 'It's for Pat-ri-cia, Nurk-u the Bad
scratched her when she was little.'

'Terrible terrible!' The bogle shook his head.
'He's a very devil, that one! All right, me young

[67]

cocksparrow, but remember, you can only ever have one flaskful—that's the rule—and I hav'ta get a favour in return.'

'Anything. I'll try very hard,' Thrump-O-moto promised.

'Good. I wants four barrels of good English beer, as high as that tree and as big as an elephant around! Agreed?'

They looked at the tree. It was as tall as the sky and golden red. Thrump-O-moto knew it was the kami tree. 'I'll try,' he said bravely but his heart went thrump.

'Good. By nightfall, mate, now don't forget! Now you comealonga-me, Pat, me girl. While Mr. Thrump-O-moto's getting me beer, we'll collect your ESP.'

Patricia looked at Thrump-O-moto. He nodded. 'You go with Mr. Charley Rednosebeerdrinker, I've got work to do.'

She obeyed. They went deeper into the wood. The ground was soft with pine needles. Here and there were clumps of Sunset Primroses and Charley Rednosebeerdrinker sang a little song and waited until the sun touched the earth. Then he began another song, soft and sweet, and he went up to certain plants, not all, and asked for their secret sap. Some agreed, some did not. 'They're very pesky, you know,' he whispered. 'When did Nurk-u the Bad catch you?'

'I think it was about three years ago,' she said. 'I don't remember exactly. He almost got Thrump-O a day or so ago but he fought him off.'

'He's lucky. Got to keep an eye out all the time for Nurk-u. He's all over—except here. Hummmmmm! This is thirsty work.' He stopped and reached under a bed of moss. In his hand now was another tankard of beer. 'That's better. Now, Pat, me girl, we've to work quick as a wink. When evening's come there's no more ESP this day.'

She followed him from plant to plant and thanked them for their essence. Soon evening came. But now the flask he carried was almost full. The elixir was golden and sparkled as though filled with diamonds and smelled of meadows and rich harvest.

'Good-oh and dinky-di! That's enough,' he said. 'Let's find O!'

They went back to the pleasant place. 'Oh,' he said, his face twisting up. 'Now wot's this?'

Thrump-O-moto was exhausted and almost in tears. 'I did my best,' he said. There were only two barrels and they were not nearly as high as the kami tree and were only as round as a sheep, not an elephant and it was Japanese beer, not English beer.

'Oh never mind, O,' Patricia said sadly. 'You did very well. Very well indeed. I couldn't even make even one cup. Never mind.'

'Hummmmmm!' Old Charley Rednosebeer-drinker tipped his top hat back on his forehead and stomped up to the first barrel and turned on the tap. The beer frothed into his mug. He drank the whole mug down. He went to the second and tried that too. 'Hummmmmm! Hard to tell from just a sip.' Another tankard from the first and another tankard from the second. 'Well,' he said reluctantly, 'it's good beer, right enough, even though you didn't do me favour proper—now did you?'

'No, that's true. Please, can I try again tomorrow?' Thrump-O-moto asked. 'I think I must be a little tired.'

'No, not tomorrerr—not ever again, Thrump-O-moto, me lad! Sorry, young feller, but a bargin's a bargin right enough.' Absently he poured another tankard and quaffed it. His nose went even redder. Then he beamed. 'Tell you wot! As you does your best, then I does me best, too. Here take me ESP and off you go with me blessing!'

They thanked him and thanked him. 'But Mr. Charley Red-nosebeerdrinker,' Thrump-O-moto said. 'What does Pat-ri-cia do with ESP, Essence of Sunset Primroses?'

'She drinks it of course. Little at a time, a dewdrop at a time, once a day at eventide. She has to say the magic words: Omm Mahnee Padmee Humm and in the Great Spirit's time, sooner or sooner ring-a-ding-dee, up she'll get and Bob's your Uncle! Thanks for the beer, mate. I—'

[72]

Charley Rednosebeerdrinker stopped. The colour went out of his face. Above him the sky began to darken. In the tops of the trees the wind began to whine. 'Sorry, mateys. I have to go. This place is not for the likes of me now. Guard the ESP, it's all you'll ever get here.' Quick as a flash he scurried away and disappeared up into his house that was built into a crab apple tree, almost part of the tree, that they had not noticed before.

The forest got darker and darker. Thrump-O-moto and the Patricia huddled closer together. He put his arm around her and she put her arm around him and held on tight to her walking stick. The sky became darker and ever darker. Winds whirled leaves and petals. They heard many a primrose calling out warnings: 'Shut your homes, hide in the ground, Muldoona, Hag Queen of the Forest, is coming.'

'Don't worry-O, I'll help all I can.' Patricia's heart quavered. 'Quick, quick, wozz us away!'

'Yes, hold on! Now: Minamoto—kazi . . . kazi . . . oh dear!' He cried out. 'I've forgotten the next word . . . the next word.'

'Quick, O! Try-O, try very hard!'

Now the wind was howling. It bent the forest. Then suddenly there was silence. And she appeared. Enormous, with eight arms like old tree limbs and such eyes and a voice that filled the whole forest.

[76]

'Give me my ESPPPP. It's not for little girls, it's mine, mine! Give it to me or I'll carry you back to Dark o' the Day!' And all around them dark evil trees were sprouting, trapping them, imprisoning them. Now there was no escape. 'Quick, my ESPPPP or I'll eat you up.'

'No, Hag Queen of the Forest. Never! It belongs to Pat-ri-cia,' Thrump-O-moto shouted back. Then he huffed and puffed but he did not grow even a little bit. 'Oh dear-O-dinimotooooh!' Again he tried and he tried but his magic wasn't any good at all. 'You can't have the ESP, it's . . .'

'It's you, or my ESPPPP, O!'

'No, no leave-O alone,' Patricia shouted.

'It's Thrump-O-moto or my ESPPPP,' the Hag Queen screeched.

'Never!'

'Never? Ha! You come along-O!' A whirlwind shrieked around Thrump-O-moto and lifted him off the ground and much as he tried his magic, it was no use at all. He went up and up and up, tumbling head over heels, up into the sky.

At once the little girl took up her stick and

attacked the tree monster with all her strength. She battered on her trunk but the trunk was solid wood and her walking stick broke into two. Helplessly she looked up into the sky. Thrump-O-moto was just a speck hurling towards the Dark o' the Day.

'All right, here you are,' she called out, trying to be brave. 'Here! You can have it!' And she offered up the flask to the evil monster who, by now, had spread all around her in thick, deadly forest that weaved and hissed menacingly.

The flask shook in her hand, not wanting to leave. All the beds of primroses quaked and moaned and wept. 'Don't give it up to her, don't give it up . . .'

'Here! You can have my ESP, Hag Queen of the Forest!' she said, completely sure she would never be able to get any more. 'But only if you bring back O.'

'I agree, but first the flask, first my ESPPPP.' Muldoona growled and reached down for the flask with an arm that was more like a twisted branch of a great old tree than an arm.

'No,' Patricia said. 'Not until O's back!'

[78]

'First my ESPPPP!' Muldoona screeched and all the forest quaked. 'Give it to me now!'

'No never!' Patricia darted away and held up the flask. 'Bring back O or I'll . . . I'll spill every drop!'

'No . . . No . . . Wait. Let's talk . . .'

'Quick, or here it goes . . .' She spilled a drop and the Hag Queen groaned.

'Wait, you win, you win, nasty little girl!' Now the gale died down and soon Thrump-O-moto began to sail back again. It seemed to take forever but then he came back to earth with a thump. Quick as a wink, Patricia cried out: 'Minamoto-kazimoto-finklemoto-Patriciamotooooooooh!'

'Ohhhhhhhhhhhhhhhh! . . .' Muldoona, Hag Queen of the Forest began to collapse. The dark and evil forest started to shrivel. A dying wind howled a last time and then she vanished. And with her went the bad trees and bad wind and the bad darkness. Once more the sun came out from the clouds. So did the insects, and all the primroses sighed with relief and congratulated them on their escape.

'Oh Patriciamoto, to be honest you did it, you did it! You're a real wizardess.' Thrump-O-moto danced

around her then
brushed the dirt and leaves
off his clothes. 'Oh, where's the flask?'

'Here, here it is,' she said, picking it up carefully. It wasn't broken and none of the precious golden liquid had spilled.

'Thank goodness!'

'But look, O.' She showed him the two pieces of the walking stick. 'I'm afraid it's busted.'

'Never mind, Ka-chan will fix it.' He put the two pieces in her belt. 'Don't worry. Quick, take the first sip! It's the first eventide, Pat-ri-cia, have the first sip.'

Trembling she took a drop. It tasted good but strange, very strange. 'Omm Mahne Padmee Humm!' All her fear and panic left her. She felt her heart slow and her legs tingle.

'Oh-O, I think it's really going to work! If only . . .'

'Have some more.'

'Oh no, just a dew drop a day, that's what Mr. Charley Rednosebeerdrinker said.' She looked all around. 'Do you think he's safe?'

Thrump-O-moto chuckled. 'He'll be like Grand-father Ten, sleeping happily.'

'Good-O! Don't you think you should wozz us home?'

His face fell almost to his sandals. 'Oh, I'd like to, Pat-ri-cia. But, to be honest, I'm not a very good wizard at all. I've forgotten the words.' Again he was almost in tears.

'Oh dear. And we are a long way from Japan-O.'

'I just don't know what to do.'

There was a sudden silence again. The sky began to darken. Again the wind began to rise. And all the flowers shivered. 'She's coming back,' they whispered. 'She's coming back, Muldoona's coming back . . .'

'Quick-O, remember the words!'

'I can't remember them. I can't, Patriciamoto. What shall we do?'

'I know,' the little girl said in a

[81]

rush, 'I'd just l—' She stopped herself just in time. I don't want to go home yet. I want to see Ka-chan and Grandfather Ten and they did say I would be home in time for tea. 'I'd just love to see Grandfather Ten and Ka-chan!' she said firmly.

There was a great rush of wind and she felt herself speeding skywards and she gasped and closed her eyes and then, suddenly, it was all quiet again.

'H ELLO, LUV!'

She opened her eyes and stretched gloriously. The sunset was beautiful and she was in her chair under the great jacaranda tree. 'Hello Dad, how're you? Had a good day?'

'Grand. I came to fetch you for tea. How're you? Mum says you've been asleep most of the day.'

'Oh but I wasn't.' She lay back a moment collecting herself. 'I had the best time I ever had, Dad. I had wonderful adventures with O and Ka-chan and drank every drop of my ESP and didn't ever miss an eventide.'

'ESP? I don't understand.'

She smiled up at him. 'You see, woz-time's different so I could spend weeks and weeks with O and Ka-chan and Grandfather Ten and still be back for tea. Their time's different.' She saw the frown on his lovely sunburned face and in his blue eyes and she knew he would not understand but that was all right too. Grandfather Ten had explained what would

[84]

happen when she went home and that you must be patient with adults, even with the best Dad and Mum in the whole wide world. 'Hummm! It's good to be home.'

'Who were you talking about, Little Girl? Dreamtime people? Ka-chan? O?'

'O—Thrump-O-moto—he's my best friend ever.'

'Some time I'd like to meet your best friend ever. He must be bonza,' he said loving her so much. 'What's he like?'

'He's . . .' Then she saw her crutches lying beside her chair and her heart jumped because she had been without them for such a long time, she had forgotten them. In her stomach was now a sudden great chill. For a moment she was quite lost.

'We've kippers for tea, remember?' he said.

'Oh yes.'

Then the little girl remembered what Grandfather Ten had said and she put away her fear and gathered herself, took a deep breath and carefully got up and stood without her crutches.

She saw the astonishment on her father's face, just as Grandfather Ten said there would be, and though she swayed and her first steps were faltering and her legs felt very strange indeed, she walked the four paces towards him and he caught her up in his arms.

'But ... but my darling little girl, how'd you do that? How'd you do that?'

'Grandfather Ten said it would be hard at first, Dad,' she said breathlessly, so happy, 'not like in their time, and I'd feel funny, my legs'd feel funny at first, but every day would be a little better. It's the ESP, Dad.'

'What's that?'

'Essence of Sunset Primroses. ESP.' She could feel his strength and warmth and his heart beating thrumpetty-thrumpetty like never before and, oh so strange, there were little tears on his sunburned cheeks. Grandfather Ten had been right again.

She hugged him and remembered what she had been told: 'Our time's not the same, Patricia, as your time,' Grandfather Ten had said. 'These things take a little longer, sometimes, and a little less, sometimes. Be patient, be brave ... and believe. Remember the magic words and come back soon.'

'I will, oh I will,' she said.

'Will what, my darling?'

'I'll go back to Japan and visit O again, Dad, and go walkabout with-O and Ka-chan and old Grandfather Ten.'

'When you do . . . will you thank them for me, thank them from the bottom of my heart.' He picked up her crutches. 'Here you are, luv.'

'I don't need those any more, Dad.' She was completely confident. 'To be honest I just need my walking stick and a little help. Would you give it to me, please, Dad?' She pointed at her chair and frowned, not seeing it. 'It's in the grass. It should be there.' She held on to him as he walked back, safe in his arms.

'There's only this old stick with some funny wind markings on it,' he said.

'That's it.' She was so happy. 'Ka-chan couldn't mend it but she said I was to keep this bit with me always and that you could make me a proper one.'

'Of course I will,' he told her, full of wonder.

And all through supper, long past the going down of the sun, far into eventide, she told them all about Nurk-u the Bad, and Muldoona, Hag Queen of the Forest, and all the adventures she had had.

Then, as always, he carried her to bed, and told her that he would come back to tuck her up and kiss her good night, as always. Her room was cosy. She snuggled into her bed, soft as thistle-down, but not as soft as the great pillows called futon that were spread on the floor for sleeping in Ka-chan's house and Grandfather Ten's house.

'Omm Mahnee Padmee Humm,' she murmured sleepily, very tired now, the little piece of stick under her pillow. 'G'night Grandfather Ten, g'night Ka-chan, g'night-O . . .'

Soft voices drifted from the kitchen. Then she heard their footsteps coming closer, as always.

'You still awake, Little Girl?'

'Yes, Dad, yes I am,' she said with a great yawn, almost into dreamtime. 'Dad'n' Mum, would you do me a favour? Would you call me Patricia and not Little Girl now? Please. To be honest I like Patricia better and soon I'll be like other girls. Please.'

'Of course, of course I will, Patricia, my darling. G'night Patricia.'

'G'night Patricia, sweet dreams.'
'G'night Dad, g'night Mum, sweet dreams . . .'

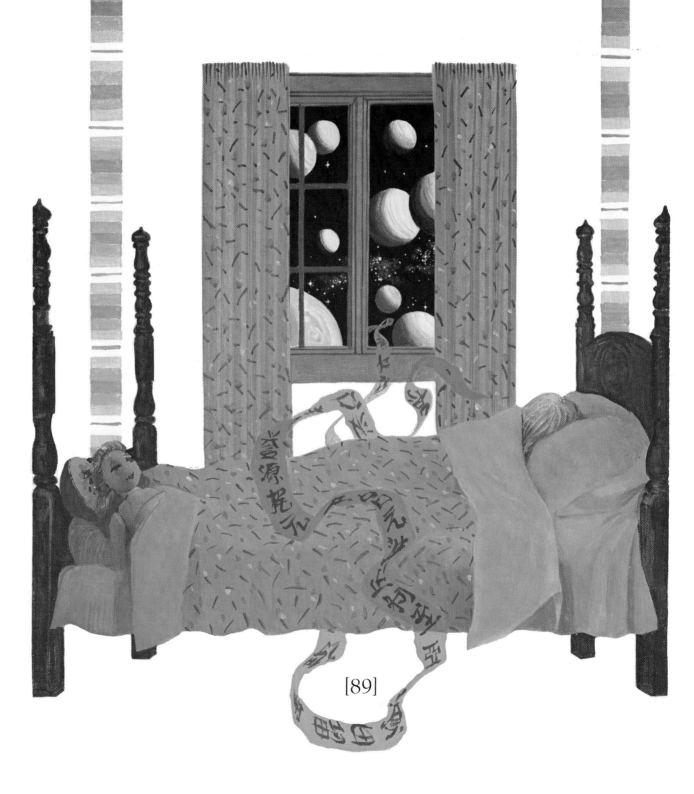

[89]

国留無保元